nickelodeon

PIRATE TREASURE HUNT!

Adapted by Frank Berrios

Based on the teleplay "Rusty Marks the Spot"
by Joe Purdy

Illustrated by Luke Flowers

 A GOLDEN BOOK • NEW YORK

T#: 539369
ISBN 978-1-5247-6795-2
rhcbooks.com
Printed in the United States of America
10 9 8 7 6 5 4 3 2 1

"**A**hoy!" Rusty greeted his friends. "Prepare to set sail, because I found something super cool! Look at this pirate treasure map of Sparkton Hills from my great-great-granddad!"

"It must be from a long time ago!" said Ruby. She read the first clue on the map:

"Find the spot the Xs mark
Across the town and in the park.
Follow the map alone or together—
It will lead you to buried treasure!"

"*Arrr,* let's go on a pirate adventure!" said Rusty.

Following the map, he led everyone into the forest.

"So, according to the map, the first X is under 'ye olde crooked tree,'" said Rusty.

"Hmm. Does anyone see a crooked tree?" asked Ruby.

Rusty, Botasaur, and the Bits looked around.
Then Ruby spotted the crooked tree!
"Awesome. This is the spot," said Rusty.
Botasaur began to dig, and before long, he
found a pile of wooden pieces!

"Look!" said Ruby. "There's a message from your great-great-granddad!" She read it aloud:

*"Finding these pieces means you're
clever and wise.
Keep searching, me mateys, to reach
your next prize."*

"I like the sound of that!" said Rusty.
"Time to bolt!"
The friends checked the map and raced off to find the next clue.

"So the next X is here in the park on some kind of big round thing," said Ruby. "Let's split into teams to search for it!" suggested Rusty.

Botasaur soon found what they were looking for.

"Of course!" exclaimed Rusty. "The old sundial is big and round. It's the perfect place for buried treasure!"

Rusty leaned against the sundial, accidentally pressing a hidden button. Suddenly, the sundial began to spin, revealing a secret chamber. Inside were three long poles.

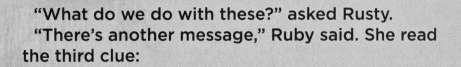

"What do we do with these?" asked Rusty.
"There's another message," Ruby said. She read
the third clue:

"Three more pieces of puzzle you've found.
Now head to the beach and be seaward-bound!"

"A puzzle?" said Rusty. "That means we're not only looking for treasure. We're actually making something, too!"

"So the last puzzle piece must be at the next X!" Ruby exclaimed.

"Come on, everyone!" shouted Rusty. "Let's load up and head to the beach!"

At the beach, Rusty and his friends ran into Mr. Higgins.

"That's one nifty treasure map you've got there!" he said. "Mind if I join in the fun?"

"Sure!" said Rusty.

Rusty found the next X and started to dig.
"I've got it!" he said, holding up a wheel.
"Looks like it's from an old wooden cart,"
Mr. Higgins observed.
"What can you do with just one wheel?"
Ruby asked.

"Hmm. One wheel can be used for steering," said Rusty. "And if we've learned anything from the other pieces, there should be another clue. There!"

Ruby read the clue:

"The pieces you've found, a new vessel make. Combine it, design it, then fair winds to the lake."

"We need to build something with all these puzzle pieces and head out onto the lake to find the treasure," Rusty said.

"Let's combine it and design it!" he told his friends. "First we connect the wood parts and the skinny poles. Then we add the old steering wheel. Put it all together and we've got our plan!"

Soon they had built a pirate ship! Then Rusty noticed another clue on the side of the ship. He read it aloud:

*"From the clues that I've given, you've
    built what I've shown.
Now add something new and make it
    your own!"*

Rusty and Ruby quickly went back to work. "Modified. Customized. Rustified," declared Rusty. "Introducing the new, improved, and fully Rustified Power Pirate Ship 1650!"

"Alrighty, Captain—let's see what this ship can do!" Ruby said.

"Prepare to bolt, matey!" replied Rusty. The powered-up ship began to zip along the water.

"The treasure should be right here!" said Ruby when they reached the spot marked on the map.

Using his Utility Glove to lower the pirate ship's claw into the lake, Rusty pulled up a treasure chest!

"Wow! The coolest treasure ever! An antique hammer!" exclaimed Rusty after they'd opened the chest. "And look, rubies . . . for Ruby! They left some cool pirate gear in here, too. Want to try it on, Bits?"

"This treasure hunt was awesome!" said Rusty.
"But it's time we headed back to shore," added
Ruby.
Suddenly, an old piece of paper fell out of the
spyglass Ruby was holding. "It's another treasure
map!" she said.

"You still want to head back?" asked Rusty. "There might be more treasure to find," said Ruby in her best pirate voice. "Full steam ahead!" "Aye, aye!" said Rusty.